Dinosaur Chase!

DINOSAUR CHASE!
A RED FOX BOOK 978 0 099 45644 5

First published in Great Britain by Hutchinson,
an imprint of Random House Children's Books

Hutchinson edition published 2006
Red Fox edition published 2007

3 5 7 9 10 8 6 4

Copyright © Benedict Blathwayt, 2006

The right of Benedict Blathwayt to be identified as the author
and illustrator of this work has been asserted in accordance
with the Copyright, Designs and Patents Act 1988.

All rights reserved.

Red Fox Books are published by Random House Children's Books,
61–63 Uxbridge Road, London W5 5SA,
a division of The Random House Group Ltd,
London, Sydney, Auckland, Johannesburg
and agencies throughout the world.

THE RANDOM HOUSE GROUP Limited Reg. No. 954009
www.kidsatrandomhouse.co.uk

A CIP catalogue record for this book is available from the British Library.

Printed in Singapore

Dinosaur Chase!

Benedict Blathwayt

RED FOX

Fin and his friends were playing games.
"Watch this!" shouted Fin.
"That's easy," yelled another dinosaur.
"I can do that!"

"Bet you can't do this!"

"Or this!"

"How about this!"

"Or even THIS...!"

Just then a gang of bullies turned up.
But they were too rough and
they spoilt the game.
"Hey!" cried Fin.
"You can't do that!"

"Oh yes we can!" said the biggest of the bullies. "We can do whatever WE want. And what can YOU do about it, with your spindly legs, knobbly ankles and bony tail? And look at those spiky claws and feeble FLUFFY arms!"

Fin's friends could see it was time to run away.

So Fin ran too.
And his spindly legs went very fast . . .

But the bullies could all run as fast as Fin.
"We can do that," they jeered.

So Fin jumped and his knobbly ankles sprang him high over a fallen tree.

One of the bullies couldn't jump…

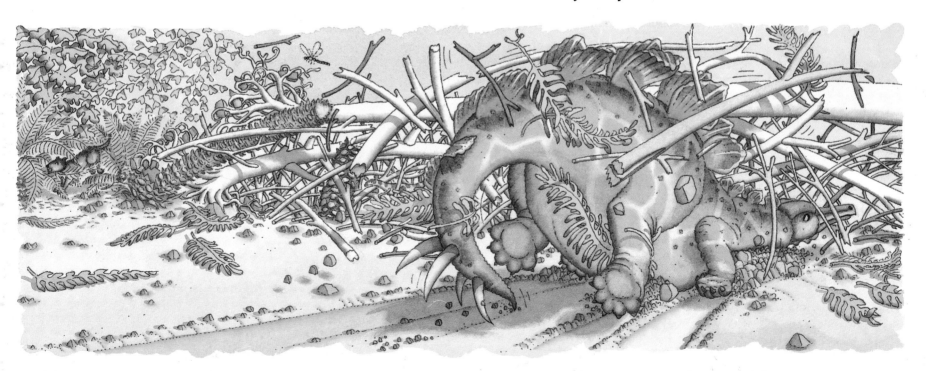

But the rest of them could.
"We can do that," they shouted.
"We can jump too!"

So Fin dived into the lagoon.

And his bony tail swished him through
the water at great speed.
One of the bullies couldn't swim...

But the other two were strong swimmers.
"We can do that," they yelled.
"We can swim too!"

So when Fin reached the other side, he ducked behind
a boulder and hid. He stayed very still, and very quiet,
until he felt sure it was safe to come out...

"BOO!"

The other dinosaurs jumped out.
"We can do that!" they laughed.
"We can hide too!"

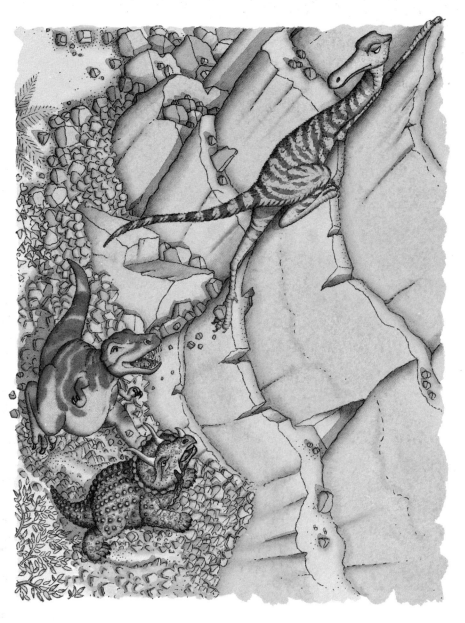

So Fin began to climb.
And his spiky claws helped him
up the steep, rough rock face.

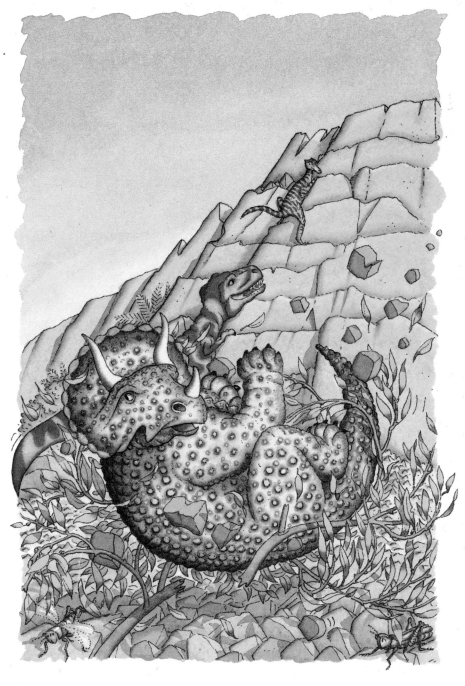

One of the bullies couldn't climb...

But the biggest, meanest,
fiercest one could.
"I can do that," he sneered.
"I can climb too!"

So Fin ran faster and faster and faster, and when
he reached the top he just could not stop…

"Help!" cried Fin as he tumbled off the mountain. But he spread out his arms and his wonderful **feathers** stretched tight in the wind.

"I can't do THAT!" roared the biggest, meanest, fiercest dinosaur of them all. And he stamped his enormous feet and swished his heavy tail until the whole mountain shook.

"I can!" cried Fin. "Look at me . . .

I can fly!"

And Fin soared through the air,
free as a bird, far above the ground.

AMAZING DINOSAUR FACTS

Dinosaurs became extinct millions of years ago ... or did they?

Some scientists think that birds are related to dinosaurs.

The oldest bird ever found, the *Archaeopteryx*, had teeth and claws,
just like a dinosaur. But was it related? Scientists needed more proof.

Then some dinosaur remains were discovered in China that had been covered in ash
from volcanoes, millions of years ago. The ash was so fine that the fossils had amazing
detail. It was quite clear that these dinosaurs had ... feathers!

So if dinosaurs became birds, how did they learn to fly? No one knows
for sure. They might have lived in trees and glided from one to the next,
like flying squirrels today. Or perhaps they used their long, strong legs to
run really fast, their arms stretched out, speeding them along. Then maybe
one day they just took off! However it happened, flying must have
been a good way to get out of trouble!

Fin is an imaginary dinosaur. He looks a bit like a dino-bird!

Perhaps Fin would
look like this as a fossil!